THE CONTEMPORARY
ART OF THE NOVELLA

THE CONTEMPORARY ART OF THE NOVELLA

BONSAI

BONSAI

ALEJANDRO ZAMBRA

TRANSLATED BY CAROLINA DE ROBERTIS

MELVILLEHOUSE
BROOKLYN, NEW YORK

FOR ALHELÍ

FIRST PUBLISHED IN SPANISH AS *BONSÁI* (ANAGRAMA).

DESIGN: BLAIR AND HAYES,
BASED ON A SERIES DESIGN BY DAVID KONOPKA

MELVILLE HOUSE
145 PLYMOUTH STREET
BROOKLYN, NY 11201

WWW.MHPBOOKS.COM

FIRST MELVILLE HOUSE PRINTING: OCTOBER 2008

LIBRARY OF CONGRESS CATALOGING-IN-PUBLICATION DATA

ZAMBRA, ALEJANDRO, 1975-
  [BONSÁI. ENGLISH]
  BONSAI / BY ALEJANDRO ZAMBRA ; TRANSLATED FROM THE
SPANISH BY CAROLINA DE ROBERTIS.
    P. CM.
  ISBN 978-1-933633-62-6
  I. ROBERTIS, CAROLINA DE. II. TITLE.
  PQ8098.36.A43B6513 2008
  863'.7--DC22
                                2008009938

BONSAI

Years passed, and the only
person who didn't change was
the young woman in the book.
                    Yasunari Kawabata

Pain is measured and detailed.
                    Gonzalo Millán

TABLE OF CONTENTS

I. MASS

In the end she dies and he remains alone, although in truth he was alone some years before her death, Emilia's death. Let's say that she is called or was called Emilia and that he is called, was called, and continues to be called Julio. Julio and Emilia. In the end Emilia dies and Julio does not die. The rest is literature:

The first night they slept together was an accident. They had an exam in Spanish Syntax II, a subject neither of them had mastered, but since they were young and in theory willing to do anything, they were willing, also, to study Spanish Syntax II at the home of the Vergara twins. The study group turned out to be quite a bit larger than imagined: someone put on music, saying he was accustomed to studying to music, another brought vodka, insisting that it was difficult for her to concentrate without vodka, and a third went to buy oranges, because vodka without orange juice seemed unbearable. At three in the morning they were perfectly drunk, so they decided to go to sleep. Although Julio would have preferred to spend the night with one of the Vergara sisters, he quickly resigned himself to sharing the servant's quarters with Emilia.

Julio didn't like that Emilia asked so many questions in class, and Emilia disliked the fact that Julio passed his classes while hardly setting foot on campus, but that night they both discovered the emotional affinities that any couple is capable of discovering with only a little effort. Needless to say, they did terribly on the exam. A week later, for their second chance at the exam, they studied again with the Vergaras and slept together again, even though this second time it was not necessary for them to share a room, since the twins' parents were on a trip to Buenos Aires.

Shortly before getting involved with Julio, Emilia had decided that from now on she would *follar*, as the Spanish do, she would no longer make love with anyone, she would not screw or bone anybody, and much less would she fuck. This is a Chilean problem, Emilia said, then, to Julio, with an ease that only came to her in the darkness, and in a very low voice, of course: This is a problem for Chilean youth, we're too young to make love, and in Chile if you don't make love you can only fuck, but it would be disagreeable to fuck you, I'd prefer it if we shagged, *si folláramos*, as they do in Spain.

At that time Emilia had never been to Spain. Years

later she would live in Madrid, a city where she'd shag quite a bit, though no longer with Julio, but rather, mainly, with Javier Martínez and with Ángel García Atienza and with Julián Alburquerque and even, but only once, and under some pressure, with Karolina Kopeć, her Polish friend. On this night, this second night, on the other hand, Julio was transformed into the second sexual partner of Emilia's life, into, as mothers and psychologists say with some hypocrisy, Emilia's second man, while Emilia in turn became Julio's first serious relationship. Julio avoided serious relationships, hiding not from women so much as from seriousness, since he knew seriousness was as dangerous as women, or more so. Julio knew he was doomed to seriousness, and he attempted, stubbornly, to change his serious fate, to pass the time waiting stoically for that horrible and inevitable day when seriousness would arrive and settle into his life forever.

Emilia's first boyfriend was dim, but there was authenticity in his dimness. He made many mistakes and almost always knew enough to acknowledge them and make amends, but some mistakes are impossible to make amends for, and the dim one, the first one, made one or two of those unpardonable mistakes. It's not even worth mentioning them.

Both of them were fifteen years old when they started going out, but when Emilia turned sixteen and seventeen the dim one was still fifteen. That's how it went: Emilia turned eighteen and nineteen and twenty-four, and he was fifteen; twenty-seven, twenty-eight, and he fifteen, still, until her thirtieth, since Emilia did not keep having birthdays after thirty, and not because she at that point decided to conceal her age, but rather because a few days after turning thirty Emilia died, and so she no longer turned older because she began to be dead.

Emilia's second boyfriend was too white. With him she discovered mountaineering in the Andes, bicycle rides, jogging, and yogurt. It was, in particular, a time of a lot of yogurt, and this, for Emilia, turned out to be important, because she was emerging from a period of a lot of pisco, of long and complicated nights of pisco with Coca-Cola and pisco with lemon, and also of pisco straight up, dry, no ice. They groped each other a lot but never arrived at coitus, because he was very white and this made her distrustful, despite the fact that she herself was very white, almost completely white, with short hair that was very black, she did have that.

The third one was, in fact, a sick man. From the start she knew the relationship was doomed to failure, but even so they lasted a year and a half, and he was her first sexual partner, her first man, when she was eighteen, and he was twenty-two.

Between the third and the fourth there were several one-night stands, spurred, as it were, by boredom.

The fourth was Julio.

In keeping with a deep-seated family custom, Julio's sexual initiation was negotiated, at ten thousand pesos, with Isidora, with cousin Isidora, who after that point was no longer called Isidora, nor was she Julio's cousin. All the men in the family had been with Isidora, who was still young, with miraculous hips and a certain leaning toward romanticism, who agreed to attend to them, although she was no longer what is referred to as a whore, a whore-whore: now, and she always strove to make this clear, she worked as a lawyer's secretary.

At the age of fifteen Julio met cousin Isidora, and he continued to meet with her during the years that followed, in the context of special gifts, when he insisted on it enough, or when his father's brutality abated and, as a result, the period came known as the period of fatherly remorse, immediately followed by the period of fatherly guilt, whose most fortunate consequence was economic generosity. It goes without saying that Julio nearly fell in love with Isidora, that he cared for her, and that she, briefly moved by the young reader who dressed in black, treated him better than the others she was with, that she spoiled him, that she educated him, in a fashion.

Only at the age of twenty did Julio begin to approach women his age as potential lovers, with limited success but enough to decide to leave Isidora. To leave her, of course, in the same way one quits smoking or gambling at the racetrack. It wasn't easy, but months before that second night with Emilia, Julio already considered himself safe from the vice.

That second night, then, Emilia was in competition with a unique rival, although Julio never went so far as to compare them, in part because there was no possible comparison and also due to the fact that Emilia turned out to become, officially, the only love of his life, and Isidora, barely, an old and agreeable source of pleasure and suffering. When Julio fell in love with Emilia all the pleasure and suffering previous to the pleasure and suffering that Emilia brought him turned into simple imitations of true pleasure and suffering.

The first lie Julio told Emilia was that he had read
Marcel Proust. He didn't usually lie about reading, but
that second night, when they both knew they were
starting something, and that that something, however
long it lasted, was going to be important, that night Julio
made his voice resonant and feigned intimacy, and said
that, yes, he had read Proust, at the age of seventeen,
one summer, in Quintero. At that time no one spent
their summers in Quintero anymore, not even Julio's
parents, who had met on the beach at El Durazno, who
went to Quintero, a pretty beach town now invaded by
slum dwellers, where Julio, at seventeen, got his hands
on his grandparents' house and locked himself up to
read *In Search of Lost Time*. It was a lie, of course: he had
gone to Quintero that summer, and he had read a lot,

but he had read Jack Kerouac, Heinrich Böll, Vladimir Nabokov, Truman Capote, and Enrique Lihn, and not Marcel Proust.

That same night Emilia lied to Julio for the first time, and the lie was, also, that she had read Marcel Proust. At first she only went so far as to agree: I also read Proust. But after that there was a long period of silence, which was not so much an uncomfortable silence as an expectant one, such that Emilia had to complete the story: It was last year, recently, it took me five months, I was so busy, you know how it is, with the courseload at the university. But I undertook to read the seven volumes and the truth is that those were the most important months of my life as a reader.

She used that phrase: my life as a reader, she said that those had been, without a doubt, the most important months of her life as a reader.

In the story of Emilia and Julio, in any case, there are more omissions than lies, and fewer omissions than truths, truths of the kind that are called absolute and that tend to be uncomfortable. Over time, of which there was not much but enough, they confided their least public desires and aspirations with each other, their disproportionate feelings, their brief and exaggerated lives. Julio confided in Emilia about matters that only Julio's psychologist should have known about, and Emilia, in her turn, turned Julio into a kind of retroactive accomplice for each decision she had taken in the course of her life. That time, for example, when she decided that she hated her mother, at fourteen: Julio listened attentively and opined that yes, that Emilia, at fourteen, had made a good decision, that there had been no other possible option, that he would have done the same, and, without doubt, if back then, at fourteen, they had been together, he certainly would have supported her.

The relationship between Emilia and Julio was riddled with truths, with intimate revelations that rapidly established a complicity that they wanted to understand as definitive. This, then, is a light story that turns heavy. This is the story of two students who are enthusiasts of truth, of scattering sentences that seem true, of smoking eternal cigarettes, and of closing themselves into the intense complacency of those who think they are better, purer than others, than that immense and contemptible group known as *the others*.

They quickly learned to read the same things, to think similarly, and to conceal their differences. Very soon they formed a conceited intimacy. At least during that time, Julio and Emilia managed to merge into a single kind of mass. They were, in short, happy. There is no doubt about that.

II. TANTALIA

From then on, they kept *follando*, shagging in borrowed houses and in motels with sheets that smelled of pisco sour. They shagged for a year and this year seemed brief to them, although it was extremely long, and after that Emilia went to live with Anita, her childhood friend.

Anita didn't like Julio, as she considered him spoiled and depressive, but nevertheless she had to allow him in at breakfast time and even, once, perhaps to demonstrate to herself and her friend that at the core Julio did not displease her, she made him boiled eggs, which were the favorite breakfast of Julio's, that permanent guest of the narrow and rather inhospitable apartment that Emilia and Anita shared. What bothered Anita about Julio was that he had changed her friend.

You changed my friend. She wasn't like that.
And have you always been like that?
Like what?
Like that, the way you are.

Emilia intervened, conciliatory and understanding. What's the purpose of being with someone if they don't change your life? She said that, and Julio was present when she said it: that life only had purpose if you found someone who changed it, who destroyed your life. It seemed a dubious theory to Anita, but she didn't argue. She knew that when Emilia spoke in that tone it was absurd to contradict her.

Julio and Emilia's peculiarities weren't only sexual (they did have them), nor emotional (these abounded), but also, so to speak, literary. On a particularly joyful night, Julio read, in a joking tone, a Rubén Darío poem that Emilia dramatized and turned banal until it became a genuinely sexual poem, a poem of explicit sex, with screams, with orgasms included. It became a habit, this reading aloud—in a low voice—every night, before shagging. They read Marcel Schwob's *Monelle's Book*, and Yukio Mishima's *The Temple of the Golden Pavilion*, which turned out to be reasonable sources of erotic inspiration. However, very soon the readings diversified significantly: they read Perec's *A Man Asleep* and *Things*, various stories by Onetti and Raymond Carver, poems by Ted Hughes, by Tomas Tranströmer, by Armando Uribe and by Kurt Folch. They even read fragments of Nietzsche and Émile Cioran.

One fine or dark day, chance led them to the pages of the *Anthology of Fantastic Literature* by Borges, Bioy Casares, and Silvina Ocampo. After imagining vaults or houses without doors, after taking inventory of the traces of unnameable ghosts, they arrived at "Tantalia," a short story by Macedonio Fernández that affected them profoundly.

"Tantalia" is the story of a couple that decides to buy a small plant and keep it as a symbol of the love that unites them. They realize too late that if the plant dies, the love that unites them will die with it. And as the love that unites them is immense and they are not willing to sacrifice it for any reason, they decide to lose the little plant in a multitude of identical little plants. Later comes the despair, the misfortune of knowing they will never be able to find it.

She and he, Macedonio's characters, had and lost a little plant of love. Emilia and Julio—who are not exactly characters, though maybe it's convenient to think of them as characters—have been reading before shagging for months, it is very pleasant, they think, and sometimes they think it at the same time: it is very pleasant, it is beautiful to read and talk about the reading just before tangling legs. It's like doing exercise.

It isn't always easy to find, in the texts, some impetus, however small, to shag, but in the end they manage to locate a paragraph or verse that, when whimsically stretched or perverted, works for them, gets them hot. (They liked that expression, to get hot, that's why I use it. They liked it almost enough to get hot from it.)

But this time it was different:

I don't like Macedonio Fernández anymore, Emilia said, shaping her sentences with inexplicable timidity, as she caressed Julio's chin and mouth.

And Julio: Me neither. I enjoyed it, I liked him a lot, but not anymore. Not Macedonio.

They had read Macedonio's story in a very low voice and talked on in a very low voice:

It's absurd, like a dream.
Because it *is* a dream.
It's stupid.
I don't understand.
Nothing, just that it's absurd.

That should have been the last time Emilia and Julio shagged. But they kept going, despite Anita's ongoing complaints and the unusual disturbance Macedonio's story had caused them. Perhaps to burnish their disappointment, or simply to change the subject, they turned exclusively to classics. They argued, as all dilettantes the world over have at some time argued, over the first chapters of *Madame Bovary*. They classified their friends and acquaintances as to whether they were like Charles or Emma, and they also argued over whether they themselves were comparable to the tragic Bovary family. In bed there was no problem, as they both made great efforts to seem like Emma, to be like Emma, *follar* like Emma, as doubtlessly, they believed, Emma shagged exceptionally well, and would have shagged even better in current conditions;

in Santiago de Chile, at the end of the twentieth century, Emma would have shagged even better than in the book. The bedroom, on those nights, turned into a shielded carriage that steered itself, feeling its way through a beautiful and unreal city. The others, the people, jealously murmured details of the scandalous and fascinating romance that was taking place behind closed doors.

But they could not reach agreement on other aspects. They were not able to decide whether she acted like Emma and he like Charles, or whether it was both of them who, without meaning to, played Charles' role. Neither of them wanted to be Charles, nobody ever wants to play Charles' role even for a brief while.

When there were only fifty pages left, they abandoned the book, trusting, perhaps, that they could find refuge, now, in the stories of Anton Chekhov.

They did terribly with Chekhov, a little better, curiously, with Kafka, but, as they say, the damage was already done. Since their reading of "Tantalia," the end was imminent and of course they imagined and even starred in scenes in which their ending became sadder, more beautiful, and more unexpected.

It happened with Proust. They had postponed reading Proust, due to the unmentionable secret that linked them, separately, to the reading—or to the lack of reading—of *In Search of Lost Time*. They both had to pretend that their mutual read was, strictly speaking, a reread they had yearned for, so that when they arrived at one of the numerous passages that seemed particularly memorable they changed their tone of voice or gazed at each other to elicit emotion, simulating the greatest intimacy. Also, Julio, on one occasion, allowed himself to declare that he only now truly felt that he was reading Proust, and Emilia answered with a subtle and disconsolate squeeze of the hand.

Since they were intelligent, they did not slow for the episodes they knew to be famous: the world was moved by this, I will be moved by that. Before starting to read, as a precautionary measure, they had agreed on how hard it was for a reader of *In Search of Lost Time* to recapitulate the reading experience: it's one of those books that still seems pending after reading it, said Emilia. It's one of those books that we will reread forever, said Julio.

They stopped on page 372 of *Swann's Way*, specifically the following sentence:

> Knowledge of a thing cannot impede it; but at least we have the things we discover, if not in our hands, at least in thought, and there they are at our disposal, which inspires us to the illusory hope of enjoying a kind of dominion over them.

It is possible but would perhaps be abusive to relate this excerpt to the story of Julio and Emilia. It would be abusive, as Proust's novel is riddled with excerpts like this one. And also because there are pages left, because this story continues.

Or does not continue.

The story of Julio and Emilia continues but does not go on.

It will end some years later, with Emilia's death; Julio, who does not die, who will not die, who has not died, continues but decides not to go on. The same for Emilia: for now she decides not to go on, but she continues. In a few years she will no longer continue nor go on.

Knowledge of a thing cannot impede it, but there are illusory hopes, and this story, which is becoming a story of illusory hopes, goes on like this:

They both knew that, as they say, the end was already written, the end of them, of the sad young people who read novels together, who wake up with books lost between the blankets, who smoke a lot of marijuana and listen to songs that are not the same ones they separately prefer (of Ella Fitzgerald's, for example: they are aware that at that age it is still acceptable to have recently discovered Ella Fitzgerald). They both harbor the fantasy of at least finishing Proust, of stretching the cord through seven volumes and for the last word (the word "time") to also be the last word foreseen between them. Their reading lasts, lamentably, little more than a month, at a pace of ten pages a day. They stopped on page 373, and, from then on, the book stayed open.

III. LOANS

First came Timothy, a rice doll who looked vaguely like an elephant. Anita slept with Timothy, fought with Timothy, fed him and even bathed him before returning him to Emilia a week later. At that time they were both four years old. Every other week the girls' parents made arrangements for them to get together, and sometimes they spent Saturday and Sunday playing tag, imitating voices, and making up their faces with toothpaste.

Then came the clothes. Emilia liked Anita's burgundy sweatshirt, Anita asked for her Snoopy T-shirt in return, and so began a solid commerce that grew chaotic over the years. At the age of eight there was the book about origami which Anita returned to her friend somewhat destroyed at the edges. Between ten and twelve they took bimonthly turns to buy the magazine *Tú*, and they exchanged cassettes of Miguel Bosé, Duran Duran, Álvaro Scaramelli, and the group Nadie.

At fourteen, Emilia kissed Anita on the mouth, and Anita didn't know how to react. They stopped seeing each other for a few months. At seventeen Emilia kissed her again and this time the kiss was a little longer. Anita laughed and told her that if she did it again, she would slap her.

At the age of seventeen, Emilia enrolled at the Universidad de Chile to study literature, because it had been her lifelong dream. Anita, of course, knew that studying literature was not Emilia's lifelong dream, but rather a whim directly related to her recent reading of Delmira Augustini. Anita's dream, on the other hand, was to lose a few kilos, which did not lead her, of course, to study nutrition or physical education. Soon she enrolled in an intensive English course, and continued for some years to study in that intensive English course.

At the age of twenty Emilia and Anita moved in together. Anita had been living alone for six months, since her mother had recently made a relationship official, for which she deserved—that's what she said to her daughter—the opportunity to start over from scratch. Starting over from scratch meant starting without children and, probably, continuing without children. But in this account Anita's mother and Anita don't matter, they are secondary characters. The one who matters is Emilia, who gladly accepted the offer to live with Anita, seduced, in particular, by the possibility of shagging with Julio in the comfort of her own home.

Anita discovered she was pregnant two months before her friend's relationship with Julio dissolved completely. The father—the *one responsible*, as was said then—was a student in his last year at the law school of the Universidad Católica, a detail she emphasized, probably because it made her mistake seem more respectable. Although they'd known each other a short time, Anita and the future laywer decided to marry, and Emilia was the witness for the ceremony. During the party, a friend of the groom tried to kiss Emilia as they danced *cumbia*, but she evaded his face, claiming she didn't like that kind of music.

At twenty-six Anita was already the mother of two girls and her husband was torn between the option of buying a station wagon and the vague temptation of having a third child (*to close the factory*, he said, with an emphasis that tried to be funny, and that maybe was, since people tended to laugh at the comment). That's how well it went for them.

Anita's husband was called Andrés, or Leonardo. Let's agree that his name was Andrés and not Leonardo. Let's agree that Anita was awake and Andrés half-asleep and the two girls sleeping the night Emilia arrived to visit them unannounced.

It was almost eleven o'clock at night. Anita did her best to evenly distribute what little whiskey remained and Andrés had to run to a nearby grocery store. He returned with three small bags of potato chips.

Why didn't you bring a big bag?

Because there weren't any big bags left.

And didn't it occur to you, for example, to bring five small bags?

They didn't have five small bags left. They had three.

Emilia thought that perhaps it had not been such a good idea to arrive unannounced to see her friend. While the skirmish lasted, she concentrated on an enormous Mexican hat that reigned over the living room. She almost left, but her purpose was urgent: at the school, she had said that she was married. In order to get a job as a Spanish teacher, she had said that she was married. The problem was that, the following night, there was a party with her co-workers and it was unavoidable for her husband to accompany her.

After so many T-shirts and records and books and even padded bras, it wouldn't be such a big deal for you to loan me your husband, Emilia said.

All her colleagues wanted to meet Miguel. And Andrés could pass perfectly as Miguel. She had said Miguel was fat, dark, and nice, and Andrés was, at least, very dark and very fat. Nice he was not, she'd thought this from the first time she'd seen him, years ago. Anita was also fat and extremely beautiful, or at least as beautiful as such a fat woman can be, Emilia thought, with some envy. Emilia was rather coarse and very thin, Anita was fat and pretty. Anita said she didn't mind loaning her husband for a while.

As long as you return him.
You can be sure of that.

They laughed heartily, while Andrés tried to capture the last pieces of potato chips from his bag. During adolescence they had been very careful with regard to men. Before getting involved in anything Emilia would call Anita, and vice versa, to ask the standard questions. Are you sure you don't like him? I'm sure, don't be uptight, stupid.

At first Andrés acted reticent, but in the end he ceded, after all it could turn out to be fun.

Do you know why rum and coke is called a Cuba Libre?

No, answered Emilia, a bit tired and thoroughly ready for the party to end.

You really don't know? It's pretty obvious: the rum is Cuba and the Coca-Cola is the United States, is liberty. Get it?

I knew a different story.

Which story?

I knew it, but I forgot it.

Andrés had already told several anecdotes in that vein, which made it difficult not to consider him insufferable. He made such an effort to keep Emilia's co-workers from figuring out the farce that he even let himself tell her to shut up. One supposes that a husband, Emilia then told herself, shuts up his wife. Andrés shuts up Anita when he thinks she should shut up. And so there's nothing wrong with Miguel making his wife shut up if he thinks she should shut up. And since I am Miguel's wife I should shut up.

Emilia stayed that way, silent, for the rest of the evening. Now not only would no one doubt that she was married to Miguel, but her colleagues would also not be too surprised by a conjugal crisis, say, two weeks in length, and a sudden but justified separation. Nothing more: no calls, no friends in common, nothing. It would be easy to kill Miguel. I broke it off in one fell swoop, she imagined telling them.

Andrés stopped the car and deemed it necessary to sum up the night, telling Emilia that it had been a very entertaining party and he really would not mind continuing to attend such gatherings. They are nice people and you look gorgeous in that cobalt dress.

The dress was turquoise, but she didn't want to correct him. They were in front of Emilia's apartment and it was still early. He was very drunk, she had also been drinking, and maybe because of that it did not seem so horrific that Andrés—that Miguel—should pause awhile between one word and the next. But those thoughts were violently interrupted the moment she imagined her voluminous companion penetrating her. Disgusting, she thought, right when Andrés came too close and rested his left hand on Emilia's right thigh.

She wanted to get out of the car and he didn't want

her to. She said to him, you're drunk, and he answered no, that it wasn't the alcohol, that for a long time he had been seeing her differently. It's incredible, but that's what he said. "For a long time I've been seeing you differently." He tried to kiss her and she responded with a punch in the mouth. From Andrés' mouth came blood, a lot of blood, a scandalous amount of blood.

The two friends did not see each other again for a long time after that incident. Anita never found out exactly what had happened, but she managed to imagine something, something that she didn't like at first and that later produced indifference, being that Andrés interested her less and less.

There was no car nor third child, but rather two years of calculated silence and a separation that, all things considered, was rather amicable, that with time led Andrés to think of himself as an excellent divorced father. The girls stayed in his house every two weeks and spent, also, the whole month of January with him, in Maitencillo. Anita took advantage of one of those summers to go visit Emilia. Her guilty mother had offered several times to pay for the trip, and though it was hard for Anita to accept being so far from her little girls, she allowed her curiosity to defeat her.

She went to Madrid, but she did not go to Madrid. She went to look for Emilia, of whom she had lost all trace. It had been difficult for her to obtain the address on Salitre Street and a phone number that seemed, to Anita, strangely long. Once she got to Barajas she was about to dial that number, but she desisted, inspired by a puerile, atavistic leaning toward surprises.

Madrid was not beautiful, at least not to Anita, to the Anita who that morning had to dodge, at the metro exit, past a group of Moroccans who were plotting something. They were actually Ecuadorians and Colombians, but she, who had never in her life met a Moroccan, thought of them as Moroccans, since she recalled that a gentleman had recently said on television that Moroccans were the great problem of Spain. Madrid seemed to her an intimidating, hostile city, in fact it was hard for her to select a trustworthy person whom she could ask about the address she had written down. There were several ambiguous dialogues between the moment she got off the metro and the moment when she finally had Emilia in front of her, face to face.

You've gone back to wearing black, was the first thing she said to her. But the first thing she said was not the first thing she thought. And she thought many things when she saw Emilia: she thought you look ugly, you're depressed, you look like a drug addict. She realized that perhaps she should not have come. She carefully examined Emilia's eyebrows, Emilia's eyes. She pondered, disdainfully, the place itself: very little floor space, a complete mess, absurd, overpopulated. She thought, or more accurately she felt, that she did not want to hear what Emilia was going to tell her, that she did not wish to know what she seemed in any case condemned to know. I don't want to know why there's so much shit in this neighborhood, why you came to live in this neighborhood full of caca, replete with cunning glances, with weird young people, with fat ladies dragging bags, and with fat ladies who aren't dragging bags but who walk very slowly. She examined, once again, carefully, Emilia's eyebrows. She decided it was better to stay quiet in regard to Emilia's eyebrows.

You've gone back to wearing black, Emilia.

Anita, you're the same.

Emilia did say the first thing she thought: you're the same. You're the same, you've kept being like that, the way you are. And I keep being like this, I have always been like this, and perhaps now I will tell you that in Madrid I've come to be even more like this, completely this.

Aware of her friend's unease, Emilia assured Anita that the two men she was living with were poor fags. Fags dress very well here, she told her, but these two who live with me, unfortunately, are poorer than rats. Anita did not want to stay as a houseguest in the apartment. Together they looked for a cheap hostel, and one could say they spoke at length, although maybe not; it would be incorrect to say they talked as before, because before there was trust and now they were linked, rather, by a feeling of discomfort, of guilty familiarity, shame, emptiness. Just before the end of the afternoon, after making some urgent mental calculations, Anita took out forty thousand pesetas, which was almost all the money she had with her. She gave them to Emilia, who, far from resisting, smiled with genuine gratitude. Anita knew that smile from before, and for two seconds it reunited them and then left them again, alone, face to face, one of them wishing that the tourist would spend the rest of the week occupied with museums, Zara stores, and little cakes with syrup, and the other one promising herself that she would not think anymore about how Emilia would use her forty thousand pesetas.

IV. SPARES

Gazmuri doesn't matter, the one who matters is Julio. Gazmuri has published six or seven novels that, together, form a series on the recent history of Chile. Almost nobody has really understood them, except maybe Julio, who has read and reread them several times.

How is it that Gazmuri and Julio come together?

It would be excessive to say they come together.

But yes: one Saturday in January Gazmuri waits for Julio in a café in Providencia. He has just placed the final period at the end of a new novel: five Colón notebooks, completely handwritten. Traditionally, his wife is charged with transcribing his notebooks, but this time she doesn't want to, she's tired. She's tired of Gazmuri, she hasn't spoken to him for weeks, that's why Gazmuri looks worn out and disheveled. But Gazmuri's wife doesn't matter, Gazmuri himself matters very little. So the old man calls his friend Natalia and his friend Natalia says that she's too busy to transcribe the novel, but she recommends Julio.

Do you write by hand? Nobody writes by hand these days, observes Gazmuri, who does not wait for Julio's response. But Julio responds, he says no, that he almost always uses a computer.

Gazmuri: Then you don't know what I'm talking about, you don't know the drive. There's a drive when you write on paper, a sound to the pencil. A strange equilibrium between elbow, hand, and pencil.

Julio talks, but what he says is not heard. Someone should turn up his volume. Gazmuri's throaty and intense voice, on the other hand, booms, works perfectly well:

Do you write novels, those novels with short chapters, forty pages long, that are in fashion?

Julio: No. And he adds, to have something to say: Would you recommend that I write novels?

What kind of question is that? I'm not recommending anything to you, I don't recommend anything to anyone. Do you think I met with you in this café to give you advice?

It's difficult to talk to Gazmuri, Julio thinks. Difficult yet pleasant. Immediately Gazmuri begins to talk entirely by himself. He talks about diverse political and literary conspiracies, and emphasizes, in particular, one idea: one must protect oneself from the cosmetologists of death. I am sure that you would like to put makeup on me. Young people like you approach old people because they like that we are old. Being young is a disadvantage, not a virtue. You should know that. When I was young I felt at a disadvantage, and now as well. Being old is also a disadvantage. Because the old are weak and we not only need the flattery of the young, we need, deep down, their blood. An old man needs a lot of blood, whether he writes novels or not. And you have a lot of blood. Perhaps the only thing you've got to spare, now that I'm getting a good look at you, is blood.

Julio doesn't know what to say. Gazmuri's strong laugh saves him, a laugh that suggests that at least part of what he just said was in jest. And Julio laughs with him; it amuses him to be here, working as a secondary character. He wants, as much as possible, to stay in that role, but to stay in that role with security he should say something, something that will earn him relevance. A joke, for example. But the joke doesn't come out. He says nothing. It's Gazmuri who says:

At this corner something very important happens in the novel that you're going to transcribe. That's why I had you meet me here. Toward the end of the novel, right on this corner, something important happens, this is an important corner. For all of this, how much are you thinking of charging me?

Julio: A hundred thousand pesos?

Julio is actually willing to work for free, even though, certainly, he has no money to spare. It seems a privilege to him to drink coffee and smoke dark cigarettes with Gazmuri. He said a hundred thousand the way he said good morning before, mechanically. And he keeps listening, he lags a little behind Gazmuri, he smiles and nods, although he would rather listen to all of it, absorb information, remain, now, full of information:

Let's say that this will be my most personal novel. It's quite different from the prior ones. I'll summarize it a little for you: he finds out that a girlfriend from his youth has died. He turns on the radio, like every morning, and hears the woman's name in the obituaries. Two first names and two last names. That's how it all begins.

All of what?

Everything, absolutely everything. I'll call you, then, as soon as I make my decision.

And what else happens?

Nothing, the same as always. Everything goes to hell. I'll call you, then, once I make my decision.

Julio walks toward his apartment, visibly confused. Perhaps it was a mistake to ask for a hundred thousand pesos, though he also isn't sure that sum would be a significant amount for a person like Gazmuri. He needs the money, of course. Twice a week he teaches Latin classes to the daughter of a right-wing intellectual. That and the remaining balance of a credit card his father gave him constitute his entire salary.

He lives on the subterranean floor of a building on the Plaza Italia. When the heat dazes him, he passes the time watching people's shoes through the window. That afternoon, just before turning his key, he realizes that María, his lesbian neighbor, is arriving. He sees her shoes, her sandals. And he waits, he calculates the footsteps and her greeting of the doorman, until he feels her coming and then he concentrates on opening the door: he pretends to have put in the wrong key, though there are only two keys on the ring. It seems that none of them fits, he says in a very loud voice, while he looks at her from the corner of his eye, and manages to see a little. He sees her long white hair, which makes her face seem darker than it actually is. Once they had a conversation about Severo Sarduy. She is not much of a reader, but she knows the work of Severo Sarduy very well. She is forty or forty-five years old, she lives alone, she reads Severo Sarduy: because of that, because two plus two is four, Julio thinks María is a lesbian. Julio also likes Sarduy, especially his essays, thanks to which he always has conversation topics with gays and lesbians.

That afternoon María looks less restrained than usual, in a dress she rarely wears. Julio is about to mention it, but he restrains himself, thinking that perhaps she finds such comments disagreeable. To forget his interview with Gazmuri, he invites her over for coffee. They talk about Sarduy, about *Cobra*, about *Cocuyo*, about *Big Bang*, about *Written on a Body*. But also, and this is new, they talk about other neighbors, and about politics, strange salads, tooth whiteners, vitamin supplements, and a nut sauce she would like Julio to try one day. The moment arrives when they run out of topics and it seems inevitable that both of them return to their own activities. María is an English teacher, but she works at home translating manuals for software and sound systems. He tells her that he just got a good job, an interesting job, with Gazmuri, the novelist.

I've never read him, but they say he's good. I have a brother in Barcelona who knows him. They were in exile together, I think.

And Julio: Tomorrow I'm starting to work with Gazmuri. He needs someone to transcribe his new novel, because he writes on paper, and he doesn't like computers.

And what's the novel called?

He wants us to talk about the title, to discuss it. A man learns from the radio that a love from his youth has died. That's where it all begins, absolutely everything.

And what happens next?

He never forgot her, she was his great love. When they were young they took care of a little plant.

A little plant? A bonsai?

That's it, a bonsai. They decided to buy a bonsai to symbolize the immense love that united them. After that everything goes to hell, but he never forgets her. He went on with his life, he had children, he got divorced, but he never forgot her. One day he finds out she has died. Then he decides to pay her homage. I still don't know what that homage consists of.

Two bottles of wine and then sex. Her small wrinkles suddenly seem more visible, despite the semi-darkness of the room. Julio's movements are sluggish, María, on the other hand, takes the reins somewhat, aware of Julio's indecision. The tremor abates a little, now it is more of a rhythmic and even sensible shudder that naturally drives the pelvic game.

For a moment Julio lingers in María's white hair: it feels like a fine yet incoherent cloth, immensely fragile. A cloth that must be caressed with care and love. But it is difficult to caress with care and love: Julio prefers to move down the torso and lift the dress. She runs her hand over Julio's ears, strokes the shape of his nose, tidies his sideburns. He thinks that he should suck, not what a man would suck but rather what a woman would suck, the woman he imagines that she is imagining. But María interrupts Julio's thoughts: Stick it in already, she says.

At eight in the morning the phone rings. Miss Silvia, from Editorial Planeta, is charging me forty thousand pesos for the transcription, Gazmuri says. I'm sorry.

Gazmuri's dryness disconcerts him. It's eight in the morning on a Sunday, the telephone just woke him up, the lesbian or non-lesbian or ex-lesbian sleeping at his side begins to stretch. Gazmuri has turned him down for the job, Miss Silvia, from Editorial Planeta, for forty thousand pesos, will do the job. Although María is not even awake enough to ask him who called or what time it is, Julio answers:

That was Gazmuri, it seems he's an early riser or very anxious. He called to confirm that we'll be starting on *Bonsai* this very afternoon. That's the title of the novel: *Bonsai*.

What follows is something like a romance. A romance that lasts less than a year, until she goes to Madrid. María goes to Madrid because she has to go, but above all because she doesn't have reasons to stay. All your chicks go off to Madrid, would have been the joke from Julio's uninteresting friends, but Julio has no uninteresting friends, he has always protected himself from uninteresting friendships. Anyway, she is not the concern of this story. The story is concerned with Julio:

He never forgot her, says Julio. He went on with his life, he had children and everything, he got divorced, but he never forgot her. She was a translator, just like you, but of Japanese. They had met when both were studying Japanese, many years before. When she dies, he thinks that the best way to remember her is to grow another bonsai.

So he buys one?

No, this time he doesn't buy it, he grows it. He gets manuals, consults with experts, sows the seeds, goes half-crazy.

María says it is a strange story.

Yes, the thing is that Gazmuri writes very well. The way I'm telling it, it seems like a strange story, even melodramatic. But I'm sure Gazmuri knew how to give it form.

The first imaginary meeting with Gazmuri takes place that very Sunday. Julio buys four Colón notebooks and spends the afternoon writing on a bench at the Parque Forestal. He writes frenetically, with feigned handwriting. At night he keeps working on *Bonsai* and on Monday morning he has already finished the first notebook of the novel. He smudges a few paragraphs, spills coffee, and also scatters ashes on the manuscript.

To María: It's the greatest test for a writer. In *Bonsai* almost nothing happens, the plot could be told in two paragraphs, a story that perhaps is not that good.

And what are they called?

The characters? Gazmuri didn't name them.

He says it's better, and I agree: they are He and She, Huacho and Pochocha, John and Jane Doe, they don't have names and maybe they don't have faces either. The protagonist is a king or beggar, it's all the same. A king or beggar that lets go of the only woman he ever truly loved.

And he learned to speak Japanese?

They met in a Japanese class. The truth is that I don't know yet, I think that's in the second notebook.

In the following months Julio devotes his mornings to feigning Gazmuri's handwriting and spends his afternoons at the computer transcribing a novel that he no longer knows to be another's or his own, but which he has resolved to finish, finish imagining, at least. He thinks that the final text is the perfect farewell gift or the only possible gift for María. And that's what he does, he finishes the manuscript and gives it to María.

In the days after her departure, Julio starts various urgent emails that nevertheless stay stuck in his drafts folder. Finally he decides to send her the following text:

> You've been in my thoughts a lot. I'm sorry, but I haven't had time to write to you. I hope you arrived well.
>
> Gazmuri wants us to keep working together, though he won't specify on what. I imagine it'll be another novel. The truth is, I don't know whether

I want to keep putting up with his indecision, his cough, the way he clears his throat, his theories. I haven't gone back to teaching Latin. I don't have much more to tell you. The novel will be released next week. At the last minute, Gazmuri decided to entitle it *Spares*. I don't think it's a good title, that's why I'm a little angry at Gazmuri, but, in the end, he's the author.

Affectionately, J.

Afraid and confused, Julio headed to the Biblioteca Nacional to attend the release of *Spares*, Gazmuri's real novel. From the back of the room he manages to make out the author, who nods from time to time, conveying agreement with the observations of Ebensperger, the critic overseeing the presentation. The critic moves his hands insistently to demonstrate that he's genuinely interested in the novel. The editor, for her part, watches the behavior of the crowd, making no attempt to appear otherwise.

Julio only half-listens to the presentation: Professor Ebensperger refers to literary courage and artistic intransigence, he evokes, in passing, a book of Rilke's, he draws on an idea from Walter Benjamin (though he does not credit the author), and he recalls a poem of Enrique Lihn's (referring to him, simply, as Enrique) which, according to him, synthesizes the conflict of *Spares* to perfection: "A gravely ill man / masturbates to show signs of life."

Before the editor can take the floor, Julio leaves the

room and heads toward Providencia. Half an hour later, almost without realizing it, he has arrived at the café where he met Gazmuri. He decides to stay there, waiting for something important to happen. Meanwhile he smokes. He drinks coffee and smokes.

V. TWO DRAWINGS

She died head-on, interrupting traffic.

CHICO BUARQUE

The end of this story should give us hope, but it doesn't give us hope.

On a certain particularly long afternoon Julio decides to start two drawings. In the first one a woman appears who is María but who also is Emilia: the dark, almost black eyes of Emilia and María's white hair; María's ass, Emilia's thighs, María's feet; the back of a daughter of a right-wing intellectual; Emilia's cheeks, María's nose, María's lips; Emilia's torso and diminutive breasts; the pubis of Emilia.

The second drawing is easier in theory, but for Julio it is extremely difficult, he spends several weeks making sketches, until he arrives at the desired image:

It is a tree on a precipice.

Julio hangs both images on the bathroom mirror, as if they were recently developed photographs. And they stay there, completely covering the surface of the mirror. Julio doesn't dare name the woman he has drawn. He calls her she. The she of he, it is understood. And he invents a story for her, a story he does not write, that he does not bother to write down.

Since his father and mother refuse to give him money,

Julio decides to become a vendor on the sidewalk of Plaza Italia. It's an efficient business: in barely a week he sells almost half his books. He is paid especially well for the poems of Octavio Paz *(The Best of Octavio Paz)* and Ungaretti *(The Life of a Man)* and for an old edition of *The Complete Works* of Neruda. He also parts with a dictionary of quotations edited by Espasa Calpe, an essay by Claudio Giaconi on Gogol, a couple of Cristina Peri Rossi novels he never read, and, lastly, *Alhué* by González Vera, and *Fermina Márquez* by Valéry Larbaud, two novels he had in fact read, and many times, but that he would never read again.

He uses some of the money from the sale for his research on bonsais. He buys specialized manuals and magazines, and deciphers them with methodical anxiety. One of the manuals, perhaps the least useful but also the most favorable for an amateur, begins this way:

> A bonsai is an artistic replica of a tree, in miniature. It consists of two elements: the living tree and the container. The two elements must be in harmony and the selection of the appropriate pot for a tree is almost an art form in itself. The tree can be a vine, a shrub, or a tree, but it is normally referred to as a tree. The container is normally a flowerpot or an interesting chunk of rock. A bonsai is never called a bonsai tree. The word already includes the living element. Once outside its flowerpot, the tree ceases to be a bonsai.

Julio memorizes the definition, because he likes the notion that a rock could be considered interesting and the diverse points made in the paragraph seem fitting. "The selection of the appropriate pot for a tree is almost an art form in itself," he thinks and repeats, until he convinces himself that essential information lies in these words. He becomes ashamed, then, of *Bonsai*, his improvised novel, his unnecessary novel, whose protagonist doesn't even know that the selection of a flowerpot is an art form in itself, that a bonsai is not a bonsai tree because the word already contains the living element.

Caring for a bonsai is like writing, thinks Julio. Writing is like caring for a bonsai, thinks Julio.

In the mornings he searches, reluctantly, for a stable job. He returns home in the middle of the afternoon and barely eats something before devoting his attention to the manuals: he tries to go about it as systematically as possible, invaded as he is by a hint of fulfillment. He reads until sleep overcomes him. He reads about the most common ailments of bonsais, about the pulverization of the leaves, about pruning, about the wire netting. He obtains, finally, seeds and tools.

And he does it. He grows a bonsai.

It's a woman, a young woman.

That's all María manages to know about Emilia. The dead person is a dead woman, a young woman, someone says at her back. A young woman has thrown herself in front of the metro at Antón Martín. For a moment María thinks of approaching the place where it occurred but she immediately represses the impulse. She exits the metro thinking about the alleged face of that young woman who just committed suicide. She thinks of herself, at one time, sadder, more desperate than now. She thinks of a house in Chile, in Santiago de Chile, of a garden at that house. A garden without flowers or trees that nevertheless has the right—she thinks—to be called a garden, undoubtedly it is a garden. She recalls a song by Violeta Parra: "The flowers of my garden should be my nurses." She walks toward the Fuentetaja bookstore, because she's made a date to meet at the Fuentetaja bookstore with a suitor. The suitor's name doesn't matter, except that en route she thinks, suddenly, of him, and of the bookstore and of the whores on Montera street and also of other whores on other streets that are beside the point, and of a movie, of the name of a movie she saw five or six years ago. That's how she starts to get distracted from Emilia's story, from this story. María disappears on the way to Fuentetaja bookstore. She moves away from Emilia's corpse and begins to disappear forever from this story.

She's gone.

Now Emilia remains, alone, interrupting the operation of the metro.

Very far from Emilia's corpse, there, here, in Santiago de Chile, Anita listens to yet another of her mother's regular confessions, her mother's conjugal problems, that seem interminable and that Anita analyzes with angry complicity, as if they were her own problems and in some ways relieved that they were not her own problems.

Andrés, on the other hand, is nervous: in ten minutes he'll receive a medical check-up, and though there are no minor indications of illness, it suddenly seems clear to him that during the following days he will receive horrific news. He thinks, then, of his daughters, and of Anita and someone else, another woman whom he always remembers, including when it seems inopportune to remember anyone. Right then he sees an old man emerge with a satisfied expression, calculating his steps, patting his pockets in search of cigarettes or coins. Andrés understands that his turn has arrived, that it's his turn for routine blood tests, and later the routine X-rays, and soon, perhaps, the routine scan. The old man that just came out is Gazmuri. They have not greeted each other, they haven't met nor will they meet. Gazmuri is happy, as he is not going to die: he leaves the clinic thinking that he is not going to die, that there are few things in the world as pleasant as knowing that you are not going to die. Once again, he thinks, I've made it by the skin of my teeth.

On the first night in the world where Emilia is dead, Julio sleeps poorly, but at that point he is already accustomed to sleeping poorly, due to anxiety. For months he's been waiting for the moment when the bonsai will rise toward its perfect form, the serene and noble form he has foreseen.

The tree follows the path marked by the wires. In a few years, Julio hopes, it will be, at last, identical to the drawing. He takes advantage of the four or five times he wakes that night to observe the bonsai. In between, he dreams of something like a desert or a beach, a place with sand, where three people look toward the sun or toward the sky, as if they were on vacation or as if they'd died unawares while sunbathing. Suddenly a purple bear appears. A very large bear that slowly, heavily approaches the bodies and with the same slowness starts to walk around them, until it has completed a circle.

I want to end Julio's story, but Julio's story doesn't end, that's the problem.

Julio's story doesn't end, or rather it ends like this:

Julio finds out about Emilia's suicide a year or a year and a half later. The news is brought by Andrés, who has gone with Anita and the two girls to the children's book fair in Parque Bustamante. Julio is at the Editorial Recrea stand, working as a vendor, a poorly paid yet simple job. Julio seems happy, because it's the last day of the fair, meaning that starting tomorrow he can return to caring for the bonsai. The meeting with Anita involves a misunderstanding: at first Julio doesn't recognize her, but Anita thinks he's faking it, that he recognizes her but is displeased to see her. She clarifies her identity with some annoyance and, in passing, points out that she's been separated for several years from Andrés, whom Julio vaguely met during the last days or last pages of his relationship with Emilia. Clumsily, to make conversation, Julio asks for details, attempts to understand why, if they are separated, they are engaging, now, in a wholesome family outing. But neither Anita nor Andrés has a good answer for Julio's impertinence.

Right at the time for goodbyes, Julio asks the question he should have asked at the start. Anita looks at him, nervous, and doesn't answer. She goes away with the girls to buy candied apples. Andrés is the one who stays, and he poorly summarizes a very long story that nobody knows well, a common story whose only peculiarity is that no one knows how to tell it well. Andrés says, then, that Emilia had an accident, and since Julio doesn't react, doesn't ask him anything, Andrés specifies: Emilia is dead. She threw herself in front of the metro or something like that, the truth is I don't know. She was caught up in drugs, it seems, although not really, I don't think. She died, they buried her in Madrid, that much is certain.

An hour later Julio receives his salary: three ten-thousand-peso bills with which he had planned to pay his expenses for at least the next two weeks. Instead of walking to his apartment he hails a taxi and asks the driver to drive for thirty thousand pesos. He repeats it, he explains and even gives the money to the driver in advance: go in any direction, go in circles, in diagonal lines, it's all the same, I'll get out of your taxi when the thirty thousand pesos are spent.

It's a long trip, without music, from Providencia to Las Rejas, and later, for the return, Estación Central, Avenida Matta, Avenida Grecia, Tobalaba, Providencia, Bellavista. During the journey Julio doesn't answer any of the cab driver's questions. He doesn't hear him.